This book belongs to:

_____

_____

_____

First published 2014 by Walker Books Ltd
87 Vauxhall Walk, London SE11 5HJ

This edition published 2015

2 4 6 8 10 9 7 5 3 1

© 2014 Lucy Cousins
Lucy Cousins font © 2014 Lucy Cousins

The author/illustrator has asserted her moral rights.

Illustrated in the style of Lucy Cousins by King Rollo Films Ltd

Maisy™. Maisy is a trademark of Walker Books Ltd, London.

Printed in China

British Library Cataloguing in Publication Data:
a catalogue record for this book is
available from the British Library.

ISBN 978-1-4063-5814-8

www.walker.co.uk

Maisy Plays Football

Lucy Cousins

WALKER BOOKS
AND SUBSIDIARIES
LONDON · BOSTON · SYDNEY · AUCKLAND

Good morning, Maisy!
What an exciting day!
Maisy is going to play
football. And all her
friends are playing, too.

Maisy gets dressed in her special football kit. She ties the laces on her boots. Don't forget the ball, Maisy!

Hello everyone! Dotty, Tallulah and Charley are on the blue team.

"Let's warm up!"

Maisy, Cyril and Eddie are on the red team.

"Go Team!"

It's time to start. The referee blows his whistle - WHEE!

Maisy is the first to kick
the ball...

FOUMPHHH!
Up it goes!

Up, UP and ...
over Cyril's head!

Now Charley
has the ball!

He passes it
to Tallulah...

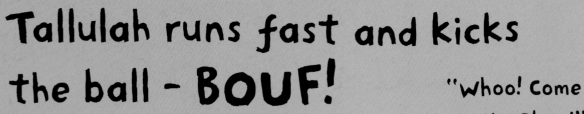

Tallulah runs fast and kicks
the ball - **BOUF!**

"Yippee for
the Reds!"

"Whoo! Come
on the Blues!"

Right into the goal.

Hooray! The blue team have scored a goal.

It's half time!

Everyone is really thirsty from all that running around. They eat some juicy oranges.

What an exciting game! Cyril passes to Maisy,

Maisy zig-zags around Charley,

Talullah tries
to tackle ...

but Maisy
kicks it
to Cyril.

Wow, Cyril's so fast!
He really wants to score
a goal for the red team.
Come on, Cyril!
You can do it!

He runs and runs and gives the ball one BIG kick into the net ... GOOOOOOAL!

WHEEEEEE! The referee blows his whistle. It's time to finish.

One goal for the red team, and one goal for the blue team. Well done everybody!

"It's a draw!"

Maisy and her friends love playing football. It doesn't matter who wins, it's just so much fun.